Me & Super Nobel

GOES BEYOND

part 1

Cornelius R. Williams

Printed in the United States of America

9798604570326

10 9 8 7 6 5 4 3 2-

EMPIRE PUBLISHING

www.empirebookpublishing.com

Contents

CHAPTER ONE

Birth of a Hero

Have you ever had a new neighbor, who just moved in right next door to you, but you had discovered their secret, I'm not talking about you discovered your neighbor is a vampire, werewolf, and some mind control zombie or that other scary movie you see at the theater.

I'm talking about something beyond that level and that is a superhero or super villain, who has the power to protect or destroy the entire human civilizations. If you don't have a neighbor living right next to you, well let me tell my story how I met a hero who have power you couldn't even imagine.

My name is Michael Dean; I live here in the state of Chicago Illinois. I know it's a tough city to live in for some people, but the reason why I live here is because I love the Colleges. I took up University of

Chicago to learn all about engineering, so I could be in the fields of space industry. I wanted to help to design spaceships.

When I had finally graduated for my engineering bachelor degree in the year 2014, I moved to the state of California to work for NASA Space Corporation. I had been working there for six years and I had the most amazing experience, working with the top best brilliant scientist.

One day working at NASA, I had to help one of the scientists take out a purple mystery rock size of car out of the spaceship. Astronauts named Adam Wilson and Dickson Spade had discovered it on planet Neptune, and they decided to bring it with them back to Earth. When I was carrying the rock, I started to hear cracking noises.

I thought to myself, rocks don't crack like that unless it's an egg. I mean, it is from another planet so it's very hard to tell what it was. Luckily the scientist and I were wearing a quarantine suit just in case if anything bad happens. The rock was quite heavy; carrying it was like holding two refrigerators together.

While the scientist and I were walking towards the experiment lab room, the rock started to move around aggressive. The scientist and I stared at each other because we both know we couldn't hold it much longer, so we quickly put it down and back away while we watch the rock move on its own.

As we both watch the rock moving, I said to myself in my mind, it must be an egg. When the rock had stop moving for couple of second, I decided to walk towards it slowly. The scientist told me to not go near that thing, because we have no clue what's inside of there. I ignore the scientist and risk it.

When I got close enough, the most stupid thing I had ever decided to do is reach my right hand and touch it. I placed my right hand on top of the mystery rock, and I was amazed because it was very warm. When the scientist and I had taken it off the spaceship, it was cold at first and now it's warm.

I told the scientist this mystery rock was warm, but when I told the scientist a giant two headed, bright greenish, spider size of a human head broke out of the mystery rock with its powerful sixteen legs. It jumped on top of me, I screamed my butt off and I tried to get it off me as I started to punch the spider.

The scientist ran and screamed for help, while I was still fighting with the alien spider from planet Neptune. The spiders sharp teeth bite right threw my quarantine suit and went inside chest. The spider injected my body with some purple liquid; it was making me so dizzy and then I passed out on the floor.

I was about to close my eyes when I fell down on the floor. I saw three U.S. military soldiers run into the science lab with their flame throwers. One the soldiers kicked the alien spider off me and across the lab center. The other two soldiers used their flame throwers to terminate the alien spider. The alien spider was burn in crisp.

As I blacked out, I heard one the soldiers yelling at me, "Sir, you okay? Sir, just hang on; you'll be okay." Twenty-four hours later, I woke up in a California hospital bed with a huge headache; my eyes were blurry, and there was a very bad pain in my chest from the spider bite and inside my mouth was very dry.

I started to look around the room and saw a woman doctor and my engineer's boss from NASA, Mr. Cody Rodriguez. They both were standing on the left side of my hospital bed. The doctor was asking me how do I feel and my respones to her was, "You look so beautiful doctor. Will you please marry me?"

The doctor started to laugh with Mr. Cody Rodriguez, because to them it was a funny response and they knew I wasn't well. The doctor told me to try to get enough rest, and so they both left out the room.

To make this story quicker, so I can begin telling you about my mystery neighbor, I stayed in the hospital for two months, when I got out scientist from NASA wanted to do experiment on me to make sure I wasn't affected by the alien spider bite that might carry radioactive poison. They couldn't believe the results, nor could I; I was one hundred percent healthy with no radioactive poison affects.

I decided to tell my boss, Mr. Cody Rodriguez, I was going to take some time off at the NASA after what happen to me. He was cool about it. He told me to take much time as I need. I decided to move back to Chicago to start my new little life. Three years later, I bought a house at Chicago Hawthorn Woods.

It was a very wonderful place to start fresh. The one thing that I noticed is somebody else just move into the same neighborhood living right next door to me on the left side. I stopped grabbing my boxes out of the moving truck I rented because my new neighbor was walking towards me to introduce himself.

Now, let me stop here for a couple seconds, so I can explain to you, the audience out there, about the world I live in.

I live in the number five parallel world where animals can do the same as a human. To those who don't understand what a parallel world is, I will explain it to you.

A parallel universe, also known as a parallel dimension, alternate universe or alternate reality, is a hypothetical self-contained plane of existence, co-existing with one's own. The sum of all potential parallel universes that constitute reality is often called multiverse. So, animals or mammals can drive a car and go to work at regular jobs like humans can in my world.

My new neighbor was some sort of a male duck, that can walk and talk like a human. My neighbor walked up to me and this is what he said, "Hello, I guess I'm not the only new person who just moved into the neighborhood. Oh, I'm so sorry; I forgot to tell you my name. My name is Nobel, I just move away from Las Vegas, Nevada."

"Nice to meet you Nobel, you can call me Michael Dean." When I told Nobel my name, he gave me a very surprised look on his face. He asked me, am I serious that my name is Michael Dean. I smiled at him and said, "Yes, I am." He yelled at me, and said, "You're the Amazing Michael Kid, the superhero."

Before I continue talking about my conversation with my neighbor, the reason why Nobel knew who I was, let's just say I forgot to tell you, the audience, I have an interesting hobby of fighting crimes over the past three years, when I just came out of the hospital. So yes, I am a superhero.

Because of that alien spider bite, I began to feel stronger and faster when I just left from the NASA science experiment lab when the scientist was doing research on my body.

The day that I notice I had powers, I was about to be robbed by three punk teenagers at night when I came back to Chicago.

One of those teenagers tried to hit the back of my head with his metal baseball bat, but I quickly dodged and punched the kid in his stomach. That kid flew above the ground and went right through the building of a meat shop. I couldn't believe what I did and saw. I just stared at my fist the whole time after my attack on the kid.

The other two teenagers couldn't believe it too. They looked at each other with their eyes popped out their heads and mouths dropped down. The two teenagers decided to run for their life, as for me, I ran to a junk yard and started to practice fighting and discovered new powers that I might be able to use in combat.

The power I discovered was night vision by staring really hard. I could fly, and had super strength. I could lift airplane. I could out run a black panther in the jungle, heal myself, and a cool part I could do is create some weird sparkling blue energy balls out of my hands that could blow up anything, like a tall skyscraper building.

When I went back to NASA to tell and show all my co- workers, they were stunned. I decided to save many lives, when their life is threatened. NASA created a special green suit for me to wear to protect my body from any deadly damage. I named myself, 'The Amazing Michael Kid'.

Nobel started to tell me how he couldn't believe I've stopped thirteen asteroids by punching them in millions of pieces that almost hit Europe, India and Asia. I told Nobel my fist still hurt from all that punching, and we both started to laugh. He said to me that we should one day hang out, and I said, of course.

I asked Nobel if he need some help to move all his stuff into his house, he said no because he barely had that much in the truck to take out. He asked me if I needed help. I really didn't need any help, but I just said, yes. I had more stuff in my truck, and Nobel and I could get to know each other more while we were working and talking.

One hour later, Nobel and I had finish putting my stuff inside my new house. After we were done moving, Nobel said it was wonderful to get know me, and to have a superhero right next door to him.

I said, "Thank you for all your help." I wished I could tip him, but he didn't want to take it. So, I just gave him twelve pack of blueberry soda.

Nobel took the sodas and headed back to his truck to unload his stuff, I decided to take a break by watching some cartoons on my tv and drink blueberry soda while I'm sitting on my couch eating a bag of hot pickle chips.

Chapter Two

Electro Magnetic Bolt

2:45 a.m., I was done putting my clothes upstairs in my bedroom and I decided to take a nice hot shower after all the work I did. I began to grab my towel, soap and shampoo out of the hallway closet upstairs.

I decided to take a shower upstairs, since there were two showers for up and down stairs because I live in a two-story floor house. I turn on the shower and set my towel on the sink counter, and put my soap and shampoo inside the shower rack. I went in my bedroom to grab my lotion on top of my dresser and my pajamas.

After I grabbed the lotion and pajamas, I noticed my TV in the bedroom was still on. Channel 16 News was on and the news reporter was talking about a super villain named, Electro Magnetic Bolt that was terrorizing the city of Chicago.

They were showing a man wearing grey technology super suit that could create electric.

This unknown villain was shooting electric bombs at the police and civilians. The police tried to shoot their pistols at Electro Magnetic Bolt, but this mystery villain's high technology super suit was too powerful to destroy. The police officers weapons were useless; even the swat team couldn't defeat this mystery villain.

I quickly threw my lotion and pajamas on my bed, went into my closet to grab my super suit that NASA scientist and engineer have created for me. I ran downstairs went out the front door and flew in the sky to head down to Chicago city. As I flew, something told me this guy might be a little tough opponent for me to take on.

Twelve minutes later, I had finally made it to Chicago city, but when I got there, the city was in chaos. It was so bad, it almost looked like the junk yard I was training at when practiced my powers. All I saw was cars blown up in pieces, buildings on fire and people lying on the ground injured

I quickly ran and helped the paramedics get the civilians and police officer on to the Paramedic truck. While I was helping the Paramedics, one of the swat team members ran up to me and started to tell me where the mystery villain had disappeared. The Swat team member said this criminal went to the Chicago Bridge.

I quickly flew straight in the air and headed to the Chicago's bridge. Three minutes later, I arrive at the Chicago's bridge and when I landed on the bridge, Electro Magnetic Bolt was standing in the middle of the bridge. Before I decided to make my move, I ask this mystery villain who is he and why he's destroying Chicago.

Electro Magnetic Bolt just stared at me for a moment and gave me a smirk like he wasn't going to tell me anything. Electro Magnetic Bolt quickly raised his left hand and shot a big electric ball out of his technology gloves. It was coming towards at me; I quickly dodged the electric ball as it blew up in the air behind me.

I look behind me after the explosion which was a big mistake, because when I turn around to see Electro Magnetic Bolt, he was in front of me. I froze and Electro Magnetic Bolt punched me in face with his right hand. Let me tell you about this mystery villains punch.

Electro Magnetic Bolt punch was so powerful; I hit the ground hard and roll across the bridge. His punch was almost like getting hit by a car. I got myself off the ground feeling dizzy after the attack by Electro Magnetic Bolt. I look at him and noticed he was laughing at me like I was no match for him.

I said in my mind, 'I learned today not to ask questions first in battle and always watch my back. I ran quickly towards Electro Magnetic Bolt like a gun bullet that's been fire out. Electro Magnetic Bolt had a surprise look on his face as he noticed I had the power of speed of light.

I swung my right hand, punch in Electro Magnetic Bolt face, and used my left punch right in his stomach. Electro Magnetic Bolt was unbalanced after my attack. After I punch him in the stomach, I did an upper cut punch using my left hand right in his chin. Electro Magnetic Bolt flew up three feet in air, and fell to the ground.

I stared at Electro Magnetic Bolt as he started to get up off the ground. I told him he should be a little more careful underestimating his opponent, and then I gave him a smirk on my face for pay back. He looked at me very angry, like a bull ready to charge at a red cape.

Electro Magnetic Bolt got off the ground still staring at me as he yelled, and launched a fully charged electro bolt. After he said that, his technology super suit exploded with so much electricity energy coming out, it blew out half of Chicago City lights. After I saw his full power, I decided to show him my full power as well.

When I'm about to use my full power against my opponent, I yelled 'Super Amazing Michael Kid.' I did it in front of Electro Magnetic Bolt and he looked at me stunned because I was glowing bright blue. He looked at me, and wondered how I did it. I'm using my own energy power, he's using technology super suit that's doing most of the work.

After we both reveal our full power, we started to charge at each other. We were blocking each other's punches and kicks, and then we begin to shoot energy bombs at one another. The Chicago's Bridge was badly damaged, if you saw how we were battling, all you could see was energy bombs blowing up everywhere on the bridge.

We were fighting each other for two hours straight. But I knew the battle was about to end. Black smoke was coming out of Electro Magnetic Bolt's super suit. He tried to shoot more electricity bombs at me, but he realized his super suit was out of power. The battery to his super suit died, from using too much power.

I smiled at Electro Magnetic Bolt and told him, "Tough luck because you should've brought an extra set of batteries." I shot one of my energy bombs out of my right hand at Electro Magnetic Bolt and I blew his super suit in pieces, while he fell to the ground knock out. The battle was over; I was the hero of Chicago once again.

CHAPTER THREE

Hanging Out with Nobel

The next day, after a long battle against Electro Magnetic Bolt from yesterday, Nobel came by my house knocking on my front door around twelve after noon. I answer the door to see what he wanted.

Nobel asked me if I could go hang out with him at the arcade zone in the city. I didn't have any plans to do today since I've already finish moving my furniture around my new house, so I told him sure. We decided to take the bus together to get to the arcade, "I'm still saving up to buy a car one day."

When we got to the arcade, Nobel and I started to play Space Invaders game, Ping Pong game, Bowling game, Laser tag game, Basketball game, Zombie Madness game, Football game and Wrestling Chaos game. We were having so much fun we forgot the world around us existed.

We both wanted to take a short break after playing all the video games, so we went to the snack bar to sit down for a moment. When we sat down at the snack bar, Nobel started ask me questions; he saw me on the news yesterday fighting against Electro Magnetic Bolt. I smiled at him and started to listen to what he thought about my battle.

This is what Nobel said about the battle. "So, Michael, I saw you on TV yesterday fighting with that villain who calls himself Electro Magnetic Bolt. At first, I thought you were going to have some struggle fighting with that guy, but you were amazing when you show your full power taking him on."

I told Nobel that he was sort of a handful, but his so call technology couldn't handle me and it shut down on him during the battle. Nobel said, "If Electro Magnetic Bolt didn't need batteries to keep his super suit going could you still defeat him?" I told Nobel, "I wasn't quite sure, I mean I could have find another way to beat him."

"Nobel, I had fought two powerful opponents the past two years. They're names were Hot Head Inferno and the other super villain was Striker 15." Nobel look at me very excited to hear my story, and how I defeated those two super villains on my own from past two years.

I began to tell my story about how I stopped those villains. I fought. Hot Head Inferno in Arizona, he wanted to get his pay back for losing the City Mayor election against Don Harris. Hot Head Inferno's real name is, Mike Jordan. He said Don Harris cheated on the election, which he did, but nobody believed him.

Mike Jordan knew a couple of friends from ITT Technical Institute School; his friends had the ability to create a technology super suit just like Electro Magnetic Bolt. The suit they were working on had the ability to create fire. After the project was finish, Mike Jordan paid his friend to take the suit to use it on Don Harris.

Mike Jordan's friends didn't know that he was going to use the suit to create a mass of destruction in the city to chase after Don Harris. He lied to his friends and told them he was going to send it to NASA for a conference. Mike Jordan destroyed, thirty percent of Arizona city just to find Don Harris.

Luckily, I was in California at Beverly Hills trying to have a little vacation, but when I saw the news, Mike Jordan or Hot Head Inferno because that's what the cops named him was destroying everything in his way. The suit Mike Jordan was wearing was gigantic because it was ten feet tall.

Anyways, I flew to Arizona and started fighting Hot Head Inferno. It was the longest battle I had ever fought in my entire life, because we had been fighting for eleven hours non- stop Nobel. The only way I knew how to beat this guy was by freezing him. I didn't have the ability to do that, but I know a place that could freeze him.

I quickly grabbed Hot Head Inferno and flew him straight to the South Pole. When I made it to the South Pole, I punched his suit in the chest so hard he fell deep in the bottom of Antarctica Sea.

A U.S. military submarine went to the bottom of the sea to look for him. When they found him, he was frozen like an ice cube.

Now let me tell you about Striker 15, his real name is Devon Mac, from Ohio. He was serving thirteen years in prison for hacking into big name technology corporations such as NASA or the U.S.

military technology. He was on the top six most wanted list by the police. He was smart and dangerous Nobel.

He only stayed in prison for three years, but he started to steal the police cameras and police body armor. Devon broke all the cameras he had stolen, and built a powerful weapon out of it that could shot electric bolt. He took over the prison by taking half the guards down and releasing all the prisoners.

The prisoners decided to obey Devon, since he helped them. Devon named himself Striker 15, because that's the name he gave the electric bolt gun he invented. The owner of the Ohio State Prison called the Ohio city Mayor to tell him what was happening in prison, and the Mayor contacted me.

When I flew to Ohio State Prison, I had to fight off one hundred-twenty prisoners just to get Striker 15. The weapon Striker 15 created, he shot me three times with it. The weapon so powerful Nobel, it knocked me out for couple of seconds. The only way I know how to beat him, using my energy blast to blow the ceiling above him.

When I shot the energy blast out of my left hand, it blew the ceiling up and everything fell on top of Striker 15. His weapon was destroyed when the rocks fell on it and he was completely knocked out. So that's my story fighting with one of the top bad boys. After I was done telling Nobel my story, he congratulated my victory.

He said, let's go see a movie, and he wanted to pay for my ticket and my snack. We went to see a scary movie called, Don't go to the swamp. The Story was about a mutated cyclops that lives in the swamp; whoever dares trespass its territory will get their skin eating by the mutated cyclops.

CHAPTER FOUR

The Prototype 5000

At midnight, Nobel and I returned home after a long fun day hanging out in the city of Chicago. I wasn't tired when I return home, so I decided to watch television downstairs in the living room.

I turned on the TV and sat down on my couch, channel sixteen news was on. A news reporter was doing an interview with a scientist who goes by the name, Philip Jefferson. He was telling the news reporter that he invented a robot and calls it, Prototype 5000. I was glued to my TV, and listening carefully what he was saying about his robot.

He started to explain to the reporter, what it's capable of doing. He said to the reporter, the Prototype 5000 robot could stop any criminals and riots. The Prototype 5000 has four laser guns, two on both of its arms and one each on its shoulders. The Prototype 5000 has night vision and X-ray vision as well.

If any criminal tried to use any heavy fire weapons to destroy this Prototype 5000, it had the ability to rebuild itself by using what he calls 'revive nanobots' that could repair it in just seconds. Little tiny robotics the size of ants fixing things, that's the new technology of the future that will change the world.

That's not all he said, he also told the reporter that if the Prototype 5000 wanted back up, it could make copies out of itself by using nanobot. He told the reporter the Prototype 5000 had the strength of ten men and the speed of a bullet. The reporter was amazed to hear the new technology that was coming soon.

I wasn't amazed. It sounded to me that Philip Jefferson was trying to get rid of all the police officers and superheroes like myself out of the city. When I looked at this guy on TV, I just had a bad feeling something was not right. This so call Prototype 5000 is not going to walk up to your doorstep and pass out girl's scout cookies to you.

I also don't believe the Prototype 5000 would save us all from any threat. What I'm trying to say is, people shouldn't always trust in technology every day of their life. I turned off the TV, and went upstairs to my bedroom to get some shut eyes.

CHAPTER FIVE

The Secret had been discovered

Two o'clock am, I was in bed sleeping until I heard a loud door shut outside my bedroom window. I quickly got out of the bed to look out my bedroom window to check to see if a burglar was outside.

I was looking to the left side and right side through my window. When I look at the left side of my window, I saw my neighbor, Nobel, standing in his drive- way. Nobel was wearing all blue suit with a blue cape tied behind him. I was thinking to myself, "Why would Nobel dress up like a superhero late at night?"

I stared at him for at least ten seconds until my answer had been revealed. Nobel shot straight into the sky like a rocket, but without a rocket suit on. He was flying on his own like I do. My eyes were wide like the size of the moon when I saw him flying. All this time, Nobel had some power and he didn't wanted talk to me about it.

I quickly open my bedroom window and I flew into the sky night to follow him, just to see where he was going. Five minutes later, Nobel had landed somewhere in back alley, where you would mostly see a large group of thugs hanging out late at night. I landed and hide behind a corner store watching him.

While I was watching Nobel for a moment, I saw an eight feet tall reptile monster walking on its two legs coming out of the back alleys shadow. This unknown creature was staring at Nobel with its dark yellow eyes, like it wanted to eat him alive. I was in shock because I didn't know this creature was hiding in Chicago all this time.

I was born and raise here in Chicago for seventeen years, how could I have missed this…this unknown creature running around and hiding in the city? I was even more shocked when the reptile monster started to talk to Nobel in English. It said, "I thought I had to hunt for my food until you came by."

The eight feet tall reptile monster started to charge at Nobel like an angry T Rex dinosaur.

I was about to run into the back alley to save Nobel, but I heard Nobel yell, "Fire punch!" His whole right hand turn into red hot lava; he punched the creature inside its chest like it was no problem.

After Nobel punched the creature, he took his fist out of the reptile chest, and the crazy part I will never forget for the rest of my life. Somehow, the creature blew up into ashes! I said to myself, "How is that even possible? There's no way I have the power to do that. Who the heck is this Nobel guy and where did he come from?"

CHAPTER SIX

Friend or Foe

After the eight feet tall reptile monster exploded into ashes, I brushed the creature's ashes off my pajamas because it was all over me and the back alley. While I was cleaning myself, Nobel called my name.

He called my name like he knew all this time I was following him. Nobel said, "It's okay, Michael, you can come out now. I'm not going to hurt you, buddy." To be honest, I was so scared at what I just witnessed Nobel do to that creature. I peed all over my pajama's pants.

I was too embarrassed to come out from the corner because I didn't want Nobel to see my pants were soaking wet. So, I had no other choice but to take my pants off, and throw them into the public trash on the right side of me. I finally came out from the corner; I started waving at Nobel just to say hi to him.

Nobel looked at me like I was crazy when he asked me why I was wearing a pajamas shirt and purple duck underwear in city. I had to think fast to come up with a good lie, so I told Nobel, "Oh...um...I was flying to get some air and I ran into a group of birds in the sky. They stole my pajama's pants." He looked at me like, "Yeah, right."

Nobel started to explain to me why he didn't say he was a superhero too and why he moved right next door to me. Nobel said to me, the reason why he didn't want me to know he had powers was because he thought I would think he was a villain spying. He also said the reason why he moved right next door to me, was to protect me.

I looked at Nobel like, what is he talking about, protecting me? I told Nobel in aggressive voice, "I don't need a babysitter to protect me from no one because I can handle myself!" Nobel said that there's a time traveler from the year 2050, who's planning to terminate me. I was quite surprised when he told me that.

I said to Nobel, "Why does a time traveler from the year 2050 want to terminate me and how do you know all about this?" Nobel said he wasn't quite sure why the time traveler wants me to be terminated, but he said a good friend of his told him. I asked him, "How does your friend know about this?"

He said his friends name is Professor Neptune; he's a scientist and engineer working for the Nevada government. He said Professor Neptune, was the one who built the time machine. I didn't want to believe it, so I gave Nobel a warning to stay away from me, or I'll have no other choice take him down.

Nobel maybe more powerful than I am, but I have a couple of friends from other countries who are also a superhero like me with the power to fight him. My superhero friends and I have a special ring we always wear that changes colors whenever one of us is in danger. Red means danger and blue means doing well.

Nobel told me this villain might be too powerful and smart for me to handle. He even told me that the reason why he followed me is he was going to ask me to join his alliance. I told him, "No thanks, so get lost because we're done here." Nobel looked at me little upset and then he flew off into the sky.

When Nobel left, my mind and heart said how stupid I was for not listening to him.

ChAPTER SEVEN

The Big Ambush

One week later, I woke up in the morning at 11:26 and went straight into the shower. After I was done taking a shower, I went downstairs to the kitchen and made me a bowl of cereal.

While I was eating my cereal at the kitchen table, I was planning on what to do today. I was thinking about Nobel too. Last week when I told him to get lost, he moved out the neighborhood. I felt kind of bad for saying that to him, I just hope he's doing okay after I yelled at him.

When I was finish eating my breakfast, I decided to put on my jogging suit. I made my decision to jog around the Chicago to get some good exercise. I'm a strange guy. I take a shower, put my underwear on and go eat breakfast, and then put on my clothes.

When I put my jogging suit on upstairs in the bedroom, I quickly ran downstairs to open my front door and I was shocked at what I saw outside. My whole neighborhood was surrounded by one hundred Prototype 5000 robots, and all of them were pointing their laser guns straight at me.

Prototype 5000 robots all said at the same time, "Terminate Amazing Michael Kid!" They all shot their laser guns at me and my house at the same time for five minutes. I was still alive after they stopped firing; lucky for me, my body is built like steel. But I was seriously hurt, I couldn't get up and my house was in chaos.

CHAPTER EIGHT

I'm from the Future

I was on lying on my back on the ground, seriously hurt. I couldn't believe my own very two eyes, Philip Jefferson walk up towards me laughing with evil smile on his face. I said in my head, "It was you."

As he stood next to my body on the right side, he said to me, "Did you miss me, Amazing Michael Kid?" I look at him like, 'what are you talking about?' He said, "Oh, don't look at him like I have no idea what's going on. When he's done telling me what this is about, it will make sense. Then, he's going to terminate me!"

Philip Jefferson said he was from the future in the year 2050. His brother Adam Butler and he wanted to invent a disease plague that could wipe out fifty percent of the human population. He said it was too overpopulated in the future; the world leaders couldn't feed the whole world.

His brother and he told the world leaders and other scientist that they could create a disease which would end world hunger by getting rid of half of human race. They hated their idea, so they fired both them from the Government Science Lab.

His brother and him still tried to work in the lab to create the new disease plague, but he said I came from nowhere in the lab, fighting them both to stop their plans. He said I kicked his brother in his stomach so hard that he fell back and crashed into the acid chemical containers that melted him alive, so he didn't make it.

He was locked up in prison for life, but he found away to escape and steal the time machine from the government lab he used to work for. He chose to come to this year, 2018, so he could finish his project before 2050 comes. He told me those Prototype 5000 were created to eliminate me, so I won't be in his way stopping his plan again.

After he told me the story, I had a big smile on my face. Philip Jefferson asked me, why do I smile? I said to him, "You didn't know that I had guest coming by to visit me. If you don't know, let's just say my ring sent a message to my friends.

TO BE
CONTINUE!

www.ingramcontent.com/pod-product-compliance
Lightning Source LLC
Chambersburg PA
CBHW051406150726
48000CB00003B/1351